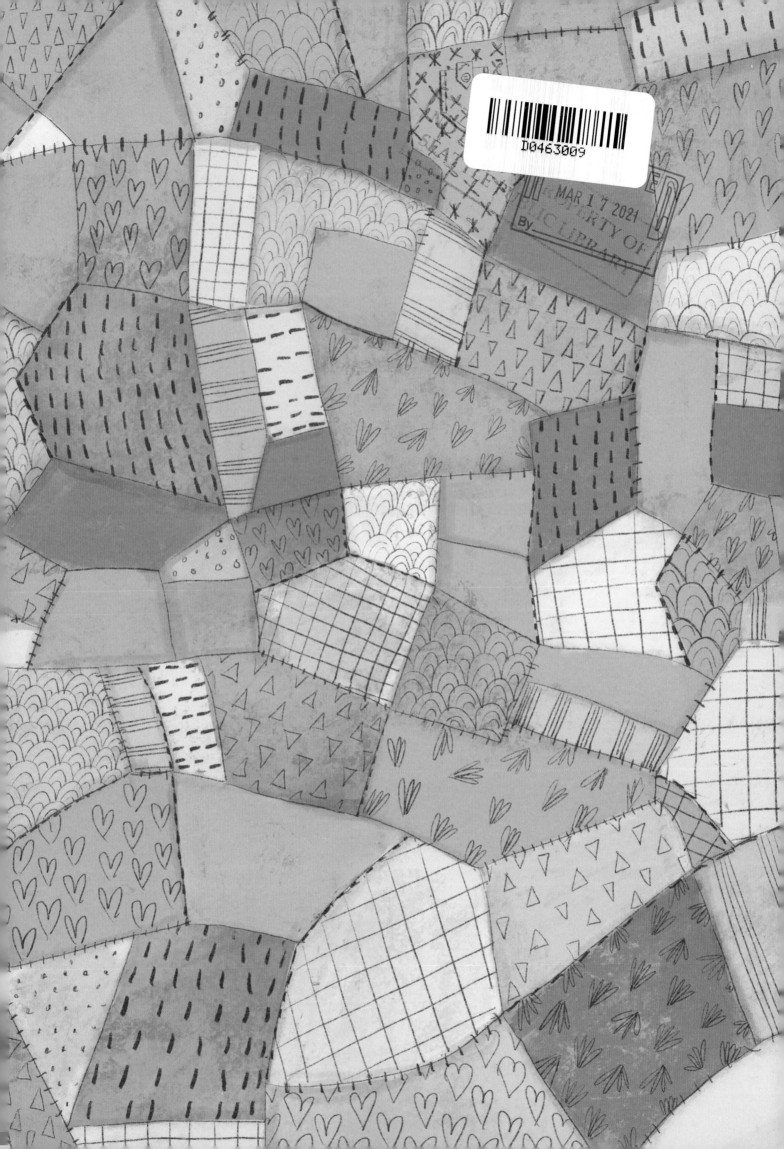

To Yasemin Uçar. AAAAH! — J.H.

For my mother, who taught me how to make friends — A.S.

Kids Can Press gratefully acknowledges the financial support of the Government of
Ontario, through Ontario Creates; the Ontario Arts Council; the Canada Council for the
Arts; and the Government of Canada for our publishing activity.

Published in Canada and the U.S. by Kids Can Press Ltd.
25 Dockside Drive, Toronto, ON M5A 0B5

Kids Can Press is a Corus Entertainment Inc. company

www.kidscanpress.com

The artwork in this book was drawn with pencils and colored digitally.
The text is set in Absent Grotesque.

Edited by Yasemin Uçar
Designed by Andrew Dupuis

Printed and bound in Buji, Shenzhen, China, in 3/2020 by WKT Company

CM 20 0 9 8 7 6 5 4 3 2 1

Library and Archives Canada Cataloguing in Publication

Title: AAAlligator! / written by Judith Henderson ; illustrated by Andrea Stegmaier.
Other titles: Alligator!
Names: Henderson, Judith, author. | Stegmaier, Andrea, illustrator.
Identifiers: Canadiana 20190213671 | ISBN 9781525301513 (hardcover)
Classification: LCC PS8615.E5225   A7 2020 | DDC   jC813/.6 - dc23

AAALLIGATOR!

Judith Henderson • Andrea Stegmaier

Kids Can Press

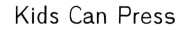

In the middle of a great forest, just outside town, there's a red house that sits next to a hidden lake. This is where the boy lives. The lake is big enough for one medium-sized whale, which is a perfect size.

The boy loves to go for walks in the forest.
It was on one of these walks that he came upon
something that stopped him in his tracks.

The alligator tried to move, but he was stuck. His foot was trapped in a twisty vine.

"Umm ..." said the boy, thinking fast.
"You must be hungry. Here, have my
tuna sandwich."
    He placed it just close enough
and jumped back.

SHWAP!

"I'll go get some more," said the boy.
He raced home and returned with a
big bag of food.

SHWAP!

SHWAP!

SHWAP!

SHWAP!

"Here's some lasagna, arugula, broccoli, onion ..."

The alligator ate everything, except the onion.

SHPIT!

He even ate the bag.

SHCRUNCH

SHCRUNCH

SHCRUNCH

The boy had brought his pocketknife to cut through the twisty vine. But how was he going to get near enough to do it?

The alligator burped, then let out
a HUGE yawn.

That gave the boy an idea.
He began to sing:

AAAAAlligator, go to sleep.

People are not good to eat.

When you wake,

You will be freeeeeeeeeeeeeeeee.

Please, please do not eat me ...

It was a brilliant idea. The alligator
fell fast asleep, and the boy used his
pocketknife to cut the twisty vine. Then
he ran home as fast as he could.

That night, he heard rustling outside his window. He got out of bed and peeked through the curtains.

BIRDS

There it was. The alligator! Waiting ...
But not in a hungry way.

"Are you lonely?"
the boy asked.

He opened the door and tossed
Theodor, his stuffy, outside.
"Please don't eat him," he said,
then quickly shut the door.

Through the window, the boy
sang the alligator lullaby. The
alligator snuggled up with Theodor
and went to sleep.

The next morning, Theodor was still there — thank goodness.

Over time, the boy and the alligator became friends.

"Let's go to town," the boy said
one day. "Please don't eat anybody."
So, off they went to the market.

The townspeople were very upset. A town meeting was called.

The mayor made a proclamation:

"NO ALLIGATORS, blah blah blah ..."

That evening, there was
a knock at the boy's door.
"I am the mayor," said the mayor.
"I have made an official proclamation.
**NO ALLIGATORS,
blah blah blah ..."**

"But he's lonely," said the boy. "And hungry."

The boy thought fast. "You know, he's actually a very helpful alligator. If you bring him your leftovers, he will eat them — no more waste."

PROCLAMATION
NO ALLIGATORS
blah blah blah
blah blah blah
blah blah blah
blah blah blah

The townspeople talked it over.

Well, we don't want a hungry alligator ...

Or lonely.

It would be sort of helpful ...

NO!

"NO!" shouted the mayor. "I'm the mayor, and I don't want any alligators!"

The boy didn't know what to do.
But then something surprising
happened ... He discovered that he
didn't have to do anything!
Every night, the townspeople
brought the alligator their leftovers.

The boy was happy. The townspeople were happy. And the alligator was happy.

The mayor, however,
was NOT happy.
   "Where is that alligator?"
he grumbled.

GRUMBLE
GRUMBLE

Whenever the mayor
came near, the alligator
found a place to hide.

The mayor searched high and low,

near and far,

here and there,

everywhere.

But he could not find the alligator, because the alligator was so good at hiding.

Over time, the alligator ate and
ate, and grew and grew.

He swam in the lake and,
sometimes, the boy let him go into
the forest alone. There was never
any problem — except once, when
a moose went missing.

But the bigger he got, the harder
it was for the alligator to hide.

The boy and the townspeople held a secret meeting.

"But the alligator needs to be near water," the boy said. He looked over at the alligator. How huge he was!

"I have an idea!" the boy exclaimed.

Together, the boy and the townspeople made a disguise.
It was a brilliant idea — a WHALE of an idea!

It did the trick. The mayor never did
find the alligator. And, curiously, nobody
could find the mayor.

SHPIT!

So the town elected a new mayor,
who wrote a new proclamation.
And things became peaceful again.

If you ever go to visit the boy and the alligator,
don't forget to learn the alligator lullaby.

AAAAAlligator, go to sleep.

People are not good to eat.

When you wake,

You will be freeeeeeeeeeeeeeeeeee.

Please, please do not eat me ...

Dream, dream, dream away.

Now you're here, you're here to stay.

Now you've found a place to beeeee.

Thank you for not eating me.

And bring some leftovers — just in case.